The YEAR of FIRE

By TEDDY JAM

Pictures by IAN WALLACE

A Groundwood Book

Douglas & McIntyre

Toronto/Vancouver

The YEAR *of* FIRE

Canadian Cataloguing in Publication Data

Jam, Teddy
The year of fire

ISBN 0-88899-154-1

I. Wallace, Ian. II. Title.

PS8569.A52Y4 1992   jC813'.54   C91-095440-2
P27.J35 Ye 1992

A Groundwood Book
Douglas & McIntyre Ltd.
585 Bloor Street West
Toronto, Ontario M6G 1K5

Design by Michael Solomon
Printed and bound in Hong Kong
by Everbest Printing Co. Ltd.

To my daughter
T.J.

To William and Constance,
Ken and Jo-Anne
and baby Caleb
with love and affection
I.W.

CHAPTER 1

IN March my mother drives me out from the city to help my grandfather make maple syrup.

His house backs into a hill so the wind can't make it cold. And on top of the hill, the maples start. Near the house just a few are left, big lonely trees with long branches that stick into the winter sky. But if you follow the hill past the barn and the pasture, there is suddenly a whole little forest of maples with a stone firepit at the bottom of the hill.

At maple syrup time my mother leaves me at my grandfather's house. His brother John comes out from town to cook for me and my grandfather while we make syrup in the old forest.

My grandfather sits in front of the boiling pan, feeding the fire. My job is to bring wood when my grandfather asks, help empty the buckets from the trees, and listen to my grandfather's stories.

Under the pan is a big fire, the biggest fire I've ever seen. One day, kneeling down and looking into it so close my face felt like it was burning, I asked my grandfather if he had ever seen a bigger fire than this.

"A bigger fire than this?" my grandfather repeated. He pushed back his hat and scratched his head. "I could tell you about a fire so big you wouldn't believe it."

"I would," I promised. My grandfather Howard always makes me promise to believe his stories.

"Okay," he said, the way he always does. "I'll tell you about a fire, the biggest I ever saw, the biggest there ever was around here."

He closed his eyes. My grandfather likes to close his eyes when he tells a story. Once I asked him why and he told me that when he closes his eyes he can see himself when he was a little boy.

CHAPTER 2

"WHEN this fire happened, this big fire, I was your age. I had just started my third year in Mrs. Brown's schoolhouse. John was a year ahead. It was fall, and one night after supper I was going to the woodshed with my father to get some kindling for the stove. It was the middle of October. There was no snow but the ground was frozen hard. The cattle and the horses were already in their barns. I used to like standing outside listening to them eat. Did you ever hear a whole barnful of animals chewing at once? I stopped to listen to them that night. And then after a little while I began to smell smoke. It was a thick heavy smell and when I turned my face to the wind it made me cough.

"My father was running up the hill. I ran after him. The smoke was coming from the Richardson swamp fields, back of the village. We couldn't

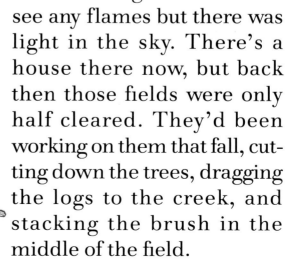

see any flames but there was light in the sky. There's a house there now, but back then those fields were only half cleared. They'd been working on them that fall, cutting down the trees, dragging the logs to the creek, and stacking the brush in the middle of the field.

"My father always blamed Richardson for the fire, though he never said so exactly, just shook his head. But that night, standing on the hill, he said, 'Richardson must have been burning brush this afternoon. Now the wind's gone up.'

"Later on Mr. Richardson said he would never have burned brush at that time of year. That was 1919, the year after the First World War ended, and sometimes returned soldiers came through, just wandering the countryside and hiring themselves out for chores. Richardson said he'd seen two men with packs earlier that day, and that they must have started a campfire, using the brush for shelter.

"We went back into the house, your great-grandfather and I. Nowadays a person would just pick up the telephone, but there was none then. My father had the next best thing, a fast horse he used to ride around the township. My mother never liked him riding at night, said he'd fall off and break his neck somewhere and die in the dark. Whenever she said that my father would just rub his hands together and start looking for his hat.

"The night of the fire was so cold you could hear the horseshoes ringing on the frozen road as my father galloped up toward the village. I sat at the kitchen table, trying to color a map for geography class.

"John was probably whittling. I never saw such a man for carving wood. Do you know he made all those puppets in the kitchen? He used to give your mother a puppet every Christmas."

My grandfather Howard looked into the fire. Sometimes his stories turned into each other, like a long braided rope connecting him to when he was a boy.

"I wanted to see the fire," my grandfather said. "I was doing my homework but I was wishing I could be out there in the middle of things.

"We had thought my father would be right back, but after an hour had passed my mother and I and John went outside. Now you could

smell the smoke right from the porch. We went running past the barns and up the hill to look.

"Back of Richardson's swamp was a section of government land, all in oak and elm trees with a bit of cedar. Everyone used to call it the forest. Some of the trees were so big around you could hide behind one on a horse. The forest was split by the creek they used to use for floating logs down to the lake.

"The fire was growing before our eyes, a wall of flame shooting up into the sky, trees exploding in great showers of sparks, so loud you could hear them right across the valley. The air was filled with birds, too, crying and cawing and cheeping like it was the end of the world."

CHAPTER 3

"WE were on our way back to the house when we heard my father riding down the road. He galloped right by us to the shed, pulled open the door, and started dragging out the cart. My mother ran to the kitchen and began throwing buckets out the door. At the time we were all scared, but later, when we'd sit around talking about the fire, everyone always started to laugh at the memory of my mother standing at the kitchen door, throwing metal pails at us. They came sailing out the door one by one, then bounced clanging down the frozen grass.

"While my father hitched up the horse, I threw the buckets and some shovels and axes into the cart. Then John and I jumped in after them. My father didn't notice us until we were halfway down the road. And then, instead of sending us back, he just said: 'Do what I tell you.'

"At the creek all the men were cutting down trees and trying to make a space wide enough that the fire couldn't jump across. The fire was burning so loud everyone had to shout. John and I were supposed to fill the buckets in the creek and carry them to the men.

"By now, the fire took up the whole sky. All the boys were there helping their fathers. John

was already so strong he could carry two buckets to my one. Bits of wood started to fly through the air like bombs, closer and closer. Everyone soaked themselves in the creek so they wouldn't catch on fire, then they kept working—until a giant branch landed in the creek with a big hiss, like a burning crocodile, and exploded all over everyone.

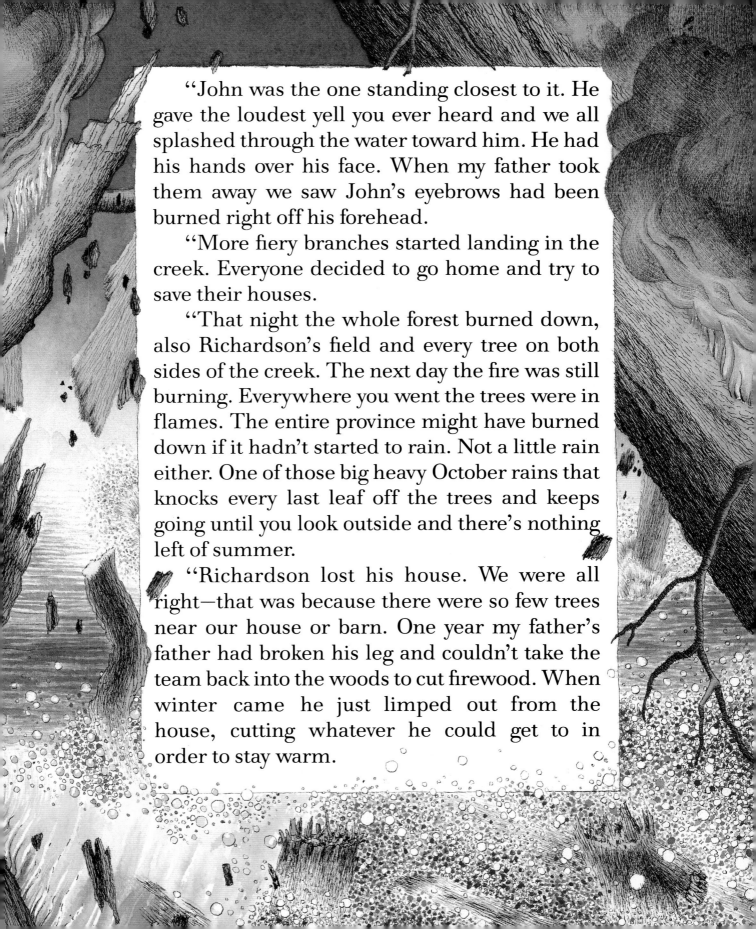

"John was the one standing closest to it. He gave the loudest yell you ever heard and we all splashed through the water toward him. He had his hands over his face. When my father took them away we saw John's eyebrows had been burned right off his forehead.

"More fiery branches started landing in the creek. Everyone decided to go home and try to save their houses.

"That night the whole forest burned down, also Richardson's field and every tree on both sides of the creek. The next day the fire was still burning. Everywhere you went the trees were in flames. The entire province might have burned down if it hadn't started to rain. Not a little rain either. One of those big heavy October rains that knocks every last leaf off the trees and keeps going until you look outside and there's nothing left of summer.

"Richardson lost his house. We were all right—that was because there were so few trees near our house or barn. One year my father's father had broken his leg and couldn't take the team back into the woods to cut firewood. When winter came he just limped out from the house, cutting whatever he could get to in order to stay warm.

"The next day after the fire my mother took us and the Richardson kids to my aunt's house in town. Then she came back to help my father. The schoolhouse burned down too. They didn't build another one until the next summer. You would have thought we'd have a whole year's holiday, but instead of that Mrs. Brown taught us our lessons in the church all winter.

"After a couple of days a crew from the army came to finish fighting the fire. By then the rain had slowed it down and, anyway, there were hardly any trees left standing. You could walk along the road or go up to the ridge behind the house, and instead of seeing woods, all of a sudden there was nothing but blackened tree trunks and burned grass, all of it still smoking. You might have thought the world had come to an end. It looked so awful you kept turning your head away.

"Two weeks later it started to snow. I was never so glad to see it. The snow piled up so high that by New Year's Day I even began to forget what was under it."

CHAPTER 4

My grandfather stopped talking. He picked up a long stick and poked at the fire. I looked at the flames as they shot up around the syrup pan. But my face got hot, so I pulled away.

While my grandfather got some more logs, I opened the knapsack and took out the lunch John had made us. It was peanut butter sandwiches and carrots. I pushed some snow off a log and lined up our sandwiches. Then I heard a loud noise and looked up. A blue jay was sitting on the bare branch of one of the maple trees my grandfather had tapped. Its feathers made me think of my great-uncle John's eyebrows in the fire. They were gray and bristly now, with big tufts of black hair that stuck out at the sides.

"Did he have to go to the hospital?"

"Who?"

"John."

"I'll tell you what happened. Mother put butter over the burns. Every single morning for months. John's eyebrow hairs got to look like porcupine quills sticking through the grease."

When we had finished our lunch my grandfather led me along the ridge at the top of the
hill. There was a big slab of rock where the sun
had melted a space to sit.

At the far end of the rock was a stump. It was
a strange stump because you could see its roots,
and they were buried in the creases of the rock.
My grandfather saw me looking at the stump,
then handed me his hunting knife. It was big
and its handle was bumpy, like my

grandfather's hand. The handle was an old
yellow piece of bone but the blade was sharp
and shiny.

"Take a piece of that root," my grandfather said.

I broke a piece off, whittled at it with
my grandfather's knife. Some of it was just
waiting to fall apart and crumbled into dark
gray dust. When I got down to the core of
the root, little yellow-red splinters came
off like toothpicks.

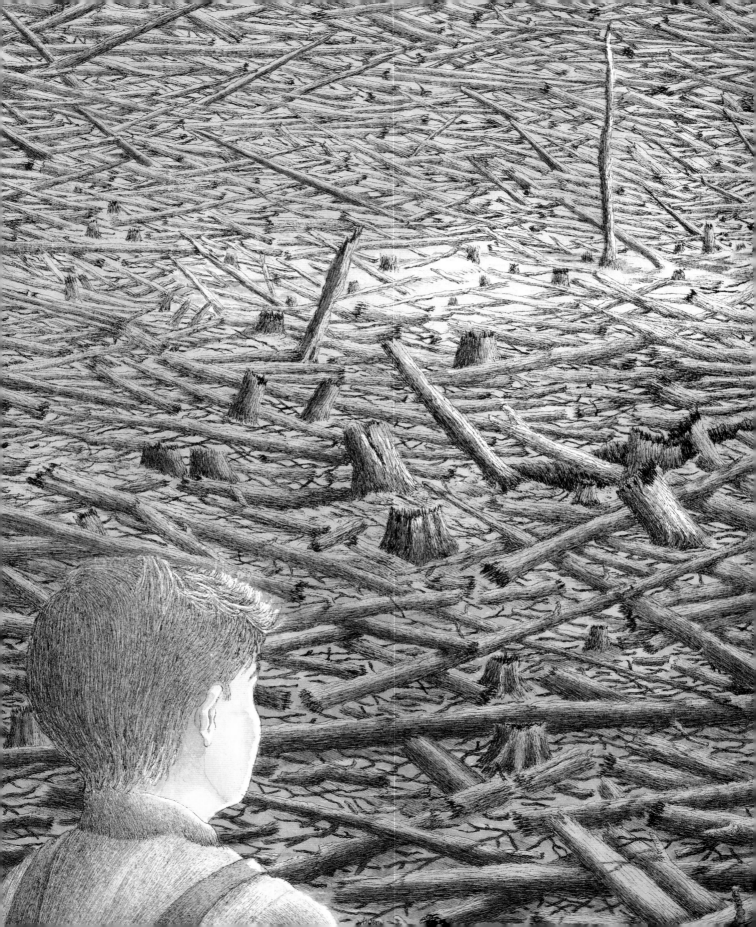

"Cedar," my grandfather said. "Richardson's swamp was filled with cedar and everyone in the country had it on their land. Used it to make fences and kindling. When spring came that year, there was still a lot of cedar standing, but all the needles were gone. Then, when the snow

melted, the trunks started to fall over. The fire had been smoldering underground all winter beneath the snow, eating away the roots, so that as soon as the deep snow melted, there was nothing left to hold up the trees. They just fell over. By the time all the snow was gone the ground was covered by ten thousand trees, lying on their sides."

I closed my eyes. Ten thousand trees. I wondered if anyone had heard them falling. I wondered what kind of noise they had made plopping into the soft snow and mud, and if they all fell at once or one at a time, like leaves in October.

"During Easter vacation we came back here with the horses and loaded the wagons with all the wood that was still good for burning. There was some cedar still standing. Those trees had been so deep-rooted that, even though the fire kept on burning under the snow, those roots held onto the only secure thing down there, the rocks.

"You see that?" My grandfather pointed to the ragged edge at the top of the stump. "I sawed that tree, right there. Used my father's bucksaw. It was the first tree I ever cut."

The blue jay had followed us from the maple grove. My grandfather reached into his pocket and threw it a crust.

"When spring came that year, the grass was greener than ever. All that black burned ground sprouted grass the way it never had before. Then after a few years the trees started growing again, so you could stand at the top of the hill and you'd see green leaves again in the valley, just the way you used to except they were brighter and didn't stick up quite so high in the sky. Now, if it weren't for these stumps, you might never know the fire had even happened."

CHAPTER 5

WE went back down to our fire. My grandfather reached into his pocket and pulled out a plastic bag with some cookies.

"What's the end of the story?" I asked him.

"The end of the story?" My grandfather looked up at the big maple trees pushing into the sun.

"First the fire burned. Then the spring came and the grass was green. Finally, after a very long time, the trees grew back. Pretty soon no one knew about the fire except for a few grandfathers. But no one asked them about it. Then there was only one grandfather who remembered it, and even he was starting to forget. Until one day when he was looking at some burning wood and a girl asked him about the biggest fire he ever saw. So he told the girl about the biggest fire he ever saw. One day there won't be anyone who remembers the fire, only people who remember the story. So you're the end of the story. Unless you tell it to someone else."

He reached into the plastic bag, took out one of the cookies and bit into it. "Don't forget to tell them about John's eyebrows. While his face was getting better he had to stay at home for two weeks. When he got bored my mother taught him how to make cookies, just like these."

Which was how the story ended, until I made my grandfather tell it to me again.